The Topsy-Turvy Bus

Juni,
The world needs your new ideas!
Anita Pazner

In memory of Stephen Gottlieb, a lifelong reader.
May all children find joy and new ideas in the
pages of books. And to my children, tasked
with making the world a better, cleaner,
happier place. - A.F.P.

To my dear friend Lizzo - C.F.

KAR-BEN PUBLISHING®
An imprint of Lerner Publishing Group, Inc.
241 First Avenue North
Minneapolis, MN 55401 USA
Website address: www.karben.com

Main body text set in Billy Infant. Typeface provided by SparkyType.

Photo Acknowledgement: Bus photo on page 30 @Uberhubris TJ Samuels.

Library of Congress Cataloging-in-Publication Data

Names: Pazner, Anita Fitch, 1966- author. | Farías, Carolina, 1968- illustrator.
Title: The Topsy-Turvy Bus / Anita Fitch Pazner ; illustrated by Carolina Farías.
Description: Minneapolis, MN, USA : Kar-Ben Publishing, [2022] | Audience: Ages 4-8 | Audience: Grades K-1 |
    Summary: "Join a busload of kids on the Topsy-Turvy Bus as it travels around the country teaching
    communities the importance of taking care of the Earth"— Provided by publisher.
Identifiers: LCCN 2021014907 (print) | LCCN 2021014908 (ebook) | ISBN 9781728419497 (hardback) |
    ISBN 9781728419503 (paperback) | ISBN 9781728444208 (ebook)
Subjects: LCSH: Environmental protection—United States—Citizen participation—Juvenile literature. |
    Sustainable living—United States—Juvenile literature. | Converted coaches—United States—Juvenile
    literature.
Classification: LCC TD171.7 .P39 2022 (print) | LCC TD171.7 (ebook) | DDC 363.72/8—dc23

LC record available at https://lccn.loc.gov/2021014907
LC ebook record available at https://lccn.loc.gov/2021014908

Manufactured in the United States of America
1-49073-49271-6/2/2021

The Topsy-Turvy Bus

Anita Fitch Pazner

illustrated by **Carolina Farías**

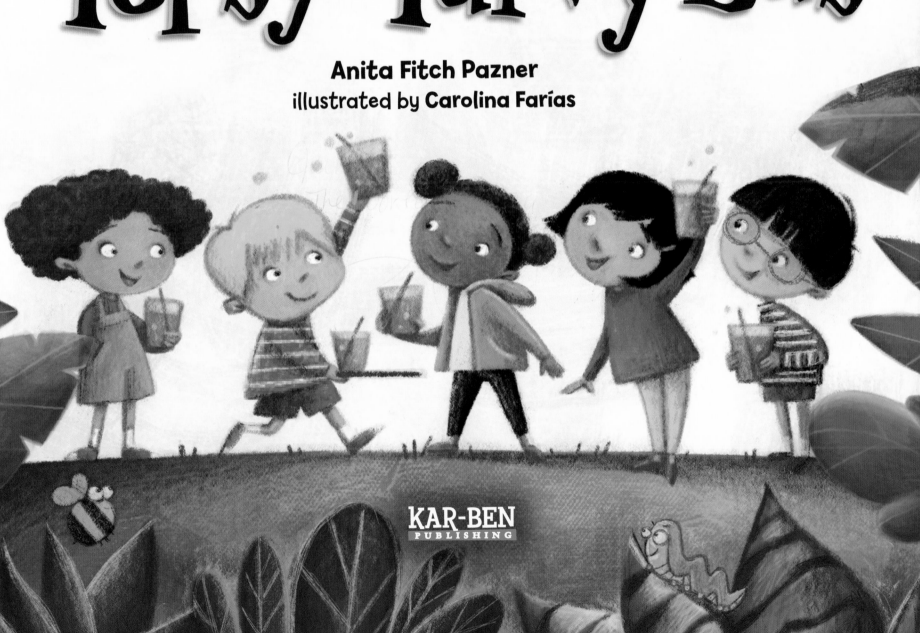

KAR-BEN
PUBLISHING

"Our planet is sad," Maddy said.

Jake nodded. "Our planet is dirty and messy."

Maddy sighed. "Our planet needs a new idea."

In school, Maddy and Jake had learned about the earth's problems.

Plastic bottles and garbage washing ashore along the oceans, littering the coastlines.

Lakes and rivers overflowing with trash and oil.

Farms use too much fertilizer to grow the same crops, year after year, exhausting the hardworking soil.

The air is filled with pollution from cars and trucks that run on gasoline.

The land hurts from drilling and mining for more oil, which is turned into more gasoline.

Animals get sick from the garbage, the fertilizers, and the pollution.

Maddy and Jake know that all this is hurting the earth.
But they don't know what to do about it.

Until . . .

The Topsy-Turvy Bus rolled into town.

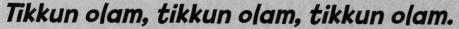

Tikkun olam, tikkun olam, tikkun olam.
Repair the world, repair the world, repair the world.

Nobody had ever seen a bus like the Topsy-Turvy Bus. It was upside down and right side up, all at the same time. And it didn't run on gasoline.

Jake sniffed the air. "No stinky bus smell."

"Smells like doughnuts," said Maddy.

The doors opened and the kids climbed inside.

"Welcome aboard!" said Wren, the bus driver.

First stop—a restaurant on the edge of town.

"Burgers and fries?" asked Jake.

"Chocolate shakes?" asked Maddy.

Wren shook her head. The Topsy-Turvy Bus wasn't there to buy food.

It had come to pick up veggie oil to use as fuel.

The lady at the restaurant was surprised to see the Topsy-Turvy Bus.

"We've come for your used cooking oil," said Wren.

"What are you going to do with all that dirty oil?" asked the lady.

"We're going to recycle it and turn it into biofuel to run the bus."

The lady shook her head. "What are you thinking?" she asked.

"We're *re*thinking," said Wren, loading the barrels onto the bus.

"Recycle, rethink, reuse, and renew," sang the Topsy-Turvy Bus as it rolled down the street.

Tikkun olam, tikkun olam, tikkun olam.

Repair the world, repair the world, repair the world.

Next stop . . . the organic farmers market.

The doors of the Topsy-Turvy Bus screeched open. Maddy and Jake hopped out.

"I grow all my fruits and veggies without sprays that hurt bugs, bees, birds, or people," said Farmer Ashley.

The kids gathered fruits and veggies to deliver to local families.

They picked peaches, peppers, and peas.

They collected colorful lettuce, cantaloupe, cucumbers, and cherries.

They bought broccoli, beets, bananas, and berries.

And packed it all in reusable bags.

They packed everything into coolers that they hauled back to the Topsy-Turvy Bus. Wren helped them unload the bike-powered blender.

Into the blender went delicious berries and pitted peaches. Maddy and Jake took turns riding the special bike.

"Smoothies for everyone!" said Jake.

"Time to go," said Wren.

Recycle, rethink, reuse, and renew," sang Wren as she drove down the street.

Tikkun olam, tikkun olam, tikkun olam.
Repair the world, repair the world, repair the world.

Next stop . . . Joel's organic worm farm.

"A farm that grows worms?" asked Jake.

"Yup," said Wren. "Nightcrawlers, Alabama jumpers, and red wigglers. The wigglers are the best garbage-eating worms in the country."

"Garbage-eating?" asked Maddy.

"Yes! Worms help make the soil healthy. Time to rethink what you know about worms. They aren't just for fishing—or scaring your brother."

"Look at all this beautiful garbage," said Wren as the Topsy-Turvy Bus rolled through the worm farm gates.

Jake and Maddy plugged their noses.

"What happens to the garbage that the worms eat?" asked Jake.

"It becomes poop," said Farmer Joel. "Some folks call it 'worm castings,'—and it's great for the earth."

"Once the worms eat up all the garbage, we put the poop back into the ground. It helps create healthy soil that can grow delicious fruit and veggies."

Farmer Joel put on his gloves and layered the bins with garbage and soil. The kids added fruit scraps from their smoothies. They all helped clamp the lid down good and tight.

"Wouldn't want these wigglers to worm their way out of the bin," laughed Farmer Joel.

When the kids returned, Jake and Maddy saw the world in a different way.

"The world is still topsy-turvy," said Jake.

"But we can make it better, cleaner, and healthier . . . one fresh idea at a time," said Maddy.

Is There a Real Topsy-Turvy Bus?

You can find a Topsy-Turvy Bus in two locations in the United States. The first is in Connecticut, the second in Michigan. Both run on biodiesel fuel consisting of reusable veggie oil. The buses were created to teach kids how to recycle, rethink, reuse, and renew our world's resources. Both buses belong to Hazon, the country's largest faith-based environmental organization. Hazon inspires environmental awareness, global health, and connection to nature and the outdoors through Jewish values. The word "hazon" means "vision." Get a glimpse of their vision for the future by visiting https://hazon.org.

Glossary

biodiesel fuel: fuel made from vegetable oil burned in diesel engines

fertilizer: a material that is added to the soil to help plants grow. Some fertilizers hurt animals and certain plants over time.

gasoline: a liquid energy source made from oil that comes from deep inside the earth. Many cars run on gasoline, which releases pollution into the air.

organic: made from nature instead of chemicals from labs

pollution: harmful materials in the air, soil, or water

recycle: taking things often thrown away, like glass bottles or plastic milk cartons, and changing them into something usable

About Tikkun Olam

Tikkun olam is the Jewish concept of repairing, healing, and perfecting the world around us through our daily actions. By changing the way we recycle our garbage, create energy, reuse our resources, renew our soil, and rethink how we treat one another, we can improve the world for all the people, plants, and animals that live on earth.

Make Your Own Compost

Turn kitchen scraps into soil that you can use for a garden or for potted plants!

What You'll Need

An empty 2-liter clear plastic bottle

A pair of scissors

A pushpin

2 cups of dirt (don't use potting soil)

1 cup of dried-out leaves (the browner and crinklier, the better!)

1 cup of torn paper, such as a paper grocery bag or a cardboard paper towel roll

Food scraps such as lettuce, coffee grounds, banana peels, and carrot shavings (avoid onions and citrus fruits)

A spray bottle filled with water

A stick or an old spoon for stirring

A tray, plate, or cookie sheet on which to set the bottle

A cheesecloth or a kitchen towel for covering the bottle

What to Do

1. Cut the top 4 inches off the empty 2-liter bottle.

2. Poke a few holes in the bottom of the bottle with the pushpin.

3. Pour the dirt into the bottle. Add the leaves, torn paper or cardboard, and food scraps.

4. Spray the material in the bottle with water to get everything moist (but not soaking wet).

5. Gently stir the material with a stick or an old spoon.

6. Put the bottle on the cookie sheet, plate, or tray. Cover it with the cheesecloth or kitchen towel. Place it in a sunny location.

7. Every few days, add more food scraps and water, and stir the material.

8. When the material decays and the bottle is full, dump it in your garden or into potted plants.